NO POETRY
LIKE WAR

Phillip Martin

ISBN: 978-1-7366378-8-3

Library of Congress Control Number: 2021902628

Cover design by: Phillip Martin

NO POETRY LIKE WAR

DISCLAIMER

The views expressed in this publication are
those of the author and do not necessarily
reflect the official policy or position of the
Department of Defense or the U.S. government.

The public release clearance of this publication
by the Department of Defense does not
imply Department of Defense endorsement
or factual accuracy of the material.

*Dedicated to the children of
the Global War on Terrorism
(GWOT) everywhere, combatants
and noncombatants, of every
nationality, both living and dead*

Mislike these not that they are so uncouth
These strident modulations of my youth

Prelude

What now I know but did not know before
Are those indifferent fields in distant lands
The boredom that abuts the glamor and the gore
The idle talk while waiting for commands
Those endless rural roads and humble faces
The sacred names of nameless places

Letter to A Hangman God on 9/11

The form you took, that second jet, you blazed
Across the azure sky, yet what amazed
Us when you hit your mark was not your force
But how you warped our time and changed our
course.
Most of us beheld your spectacle of planes
That day from far away and on TV
(Warm frozen children hypnotized were we)
And something of that stillness still remains.
It kills to think of how it could have been
Of worlds that weren't we dream that we remem-
ber.
But now, patrolling Eden, once again,
We hope that it's not us whom you'll dismember.
Though we know we can't escape you, on we go
Et in Arcadia, you sing, *ego*

No Poetry Like War

But I still hear her out the helicopter door
She weeps and bleeds white phosphorus and wine
Incandescent and incarnadine
She sings there is no poetry like war
There is no poetry like war she sings
She sings there is no poetry like war

Leave No Note

Leave no note, for letters lead to zero.
Hope your neck snaps at the proper angle.
Dangle down you fire fangled hero,
You, great satan's reconstructive angel

You, star-spangled man at last twilight cry,
Your flesh off-shuffled finally free of sin,
Fly fugue helictical, you cannot die
You vortex immaterial within

The Garden of Fire

I buried this nightmare in the garden of fire.
In the long night of a long year
And I went on my way
Nightmare trees—at first—don't like the day
But gradually their fear of daylight goes away

His face hung from a branch in the pine nut tree.
A skull, unmasked, lost to its visage baked
Bone white below in the blank light
Stripped of its self-assured smile that faked
Mor into thinking things were alright—
Gathering firewood at night? Trust me—
His face hung like a rag in the pine nut tree
These visions of the garden play, replay
Darkness grafts itself to me, cloaked in day

I buried his face in the fire garden. Was it fear?
I buried us in the long night of a long year.
I'll be the water in your Nalgene bottle.
I'll be the yoga mat in your car's back seat.
Can any war that lasts this long end in defeat?

But now it seems I have a fire orchard
Her fruits are heaving, tasteless, tortured
We have fallen from so many gardens.
What hellfire doesn't burn it hardens

At Dusk Come Hydras

At dusk come hydras from the minarets
Each static-stitched and staggering from its lair
Each ululating voice a voice begets
Crackling mournfully through the valley air.
I see her in an alley softly tread
And then she strides across the valley floor
As shadows with the fragrant woodsmoke spread
She whispers that my fictions are no more.
Her mournful hydras never sleep, she says,
Her minarets will never cease to call:
Annihilation sings us all to bed.
She blazes, fades as star clusters fall.
I still hear the music that she made
An undersong that I cannot evade

Aleksander Kheyl

The dome upon the mosque was green as life
As if this unknown god took nature for his wife
Before the storm he still remembers well
The verdant haven of Sekander Kheyl.
The birds chirped of the nimbus from the trees
That swayed amid the deadly valley's breeze
Those birds they gladly sang where they were sent
And from that place with song they gladly went
Each little throat a pipe that played for Fate
Each tiny voice a thread for Her to weave
Into the carpet She had God create
From which all songs come in, to which all leave.
The language of those birds he did not know
Back to that village he will never go

Ghazni's Devil

I hear the jingling bells her hooves drag through
The powder dust. Her rags by starlight smoke
And bleed a lurid pomegranate hue
Across her lapis breasts and heart. She woke
To stalk the ruined towers and the walls,
The labyrinthine desert walks and ways
And aches to slake her lust on them she mauls,
The lions and the lambs lost in her maze.

Across the town a cooking fire glows
Those tusks, black eyes and poppy lips, she peers
From her *qalat* towards the road—she smears
My hands with henna gently, no one knows.
In dreams she visits from Afghanistan,
Ghazni's devil with her watering can

I See Her or "Yallah, Yallah!" ("Let's Go!")

I see her eating melons in the field
Some children fetch her water from the well
She murmurs that the damned will never yield
And through a grape hut wanders back to hell.
For just one moment close your eyes and peer,
She sings, *Beyond your mirror you are free.*
For only in your blindness will you hear,
And only when you listen will you see.
She sings, *No dream of war was seen through horn*
Through ivory gates we dream and wake, reborn.
We were sent by God and by God taken
His anointed and his godforsaken

A Letter Home

The phantoms of these listless afternoons
Have wrenched from me again some gnarled runes
That no one in the world but you would choose
To waste her precious moments to peruse.
For you know well the fruits of this decryption
No prophecy pellucid, no great prescription.
(The twisted issue of a brain diseased
Can only leave a hopeful soul displeased.)
But if these glyphs should happen to divine
Some fragment of the furnace world ahead
That makes your life more bearable than mine
Then I am happy that you read. Hagridden,
The claws of furies carve my words.
I am no seer of guts and sticks and birds

JBo

Sometimes Jeremie comes back to me in dreams.
He's in full kit, in the jungle green BDUs
We wore on our tour with the 2nd Kandak کنډک,
He's wearing his Saint Christopher medal for para-
troopers,
Despite the fact that lightning struck him— now
that's faith—and his Texas ballcap.
He's even soaking wet still, from that canal in War-
dak,
And those rivers we crossed in Paktia,
With all that shit on our backs,
Burdens of lithium and lead (and Cliff bars too),
So I know it's really him

He's the same Jeremie Border I knew
Except with one difference:
He has the head of a Belgian Malinois.
Still, he has the same soulful eyes and gaze
And the same earnest voice with the trace of a Texas
accent
And the same warm, inclusive but ironic smile that
made everyone
Feel appreciated, respected yet slightly dominated
by him,
Like everyone had a feeling he was going to be the
boss one day,
And quietly celebrated

Because they knew he was the best,
And they were with him
But there he is, in full kit, with his FN SCAR,
Bravo 2,
With the head of a canine, one of the κῠνοκέφᾰλοι,
like Saint Christopher himself,
Waiting for me to make my move.
And there in full kit he says to me the refrains he'd
say to me:
*Phil, how many languages do you speak—how the fuck
do I outrank you?*
Phil, put on a fucking shirt,
You're making me feel like I have to go work out.
Phil, Brother, you can't die tonight,
Jason will kill me

If there are ghosts and spirits
(Which I know now that there are)
Then Jeremie walks somewhere, one of the good,
The kind of ghost this world needs,
Who stayed behind because that's what the best do,
Deferring heaven's orders to help us.
I don't know (yet) if he's in Batur Village in Ghazni
with Jon
I don't know if he's on Border LZ in Okinawa
I don't know if he's somewhere in Texas, maybe on a
quiet football field in Mesquite at dawn.
Hell, maybe he's in Manila drinking a cold beer with
Manny Pacquiao.

But I do know that if you see him

You are blessed
The same way that we who knew him were blessed,
Blessed to have known JBo,
To still know him,
The kind of man you want with you
In the devil's labyrinth
On the morning God takes you home

Batur Village

The daytime moon is alien in the sky
Its blue is blank and summer's heavy heat
Is too. We sit around, we do not cry,
Death baffles boredom, boredom numbs defeat

Some demon chatters Pashto in a tree
One rides a tractor, wearing neon silk
A third drinks tea and naps, then eyes with glee
A starving cow whose udders have no milk

You need not look beneath the arabesque and infra-
red
To see his handsome face, his bullet-shattered teeth

Just lay me down, and tell me when it's over
Wrap me up, and fly me home through Dover

For SSG Jeremie S. Border and SSG Jonathan P. Schmidt
KIA 01 September, 2012
RIP

You Leave to Us

You leave to us the killing and the breaking
You leave to us the bleeding and the dying
You leave to us the funerals and aching
You leave to us the burials and crying

We'll Go

We'll go into your cage and feed your wars

Yet We Are Grateful

Yet we are grateful we will never know
That we will never know that great despair
Of knowing that we had the chance to go —
And didn't — of knowing that we were not there

No curse can cut you like that silent stare
Of one who knows that you were never there

Why?

So far outside the wire with my friends
Why do I hope the nightmare never ends?

Nostalgia's Gravity

If anything of ours in Khost still stands
I do not know. But I still feel the glow
That softly warmed the North Waziri sands
When in those summer mornings we would go

A thunder stirs inside, the soul's winds blow
Our tears are delicate and dry and slow,
They dust your garden graves like burnpit ash,
Like Gardez snow

Emerald Moon

The torrid afternoons in mountain towns
The calls to prayer and other haunting sounds
You never smoked Pine Lights all afternoon,
Smelled perfumed wood and spices, charred flesh,
hair.
You never knew our emerald empress moon
Her 47s scudding through night's air
Thudding softly past the thunder to our zone,
So far out, yet never were we less alone.
The truth of all these things is plain though.
These vigils we have bled, these songs we've sung,
It is the mingled yarn, the glad and sad, a rainbow
Rising through the summer dust and dung

Sunrise Prayer at Sharana

Before the sun has risen in the east
She takes her daily bread in peace
Before the dancing and the shake
Before the passing of the snake
Before her world is once again at stake
Before her mother is awake

Transfixion

There was a threshold that she could not cross
For passing it would mean a certain loss
Yet from our sun one day she turned away
And to an inward sun she made her way
And as she traipsed beyond that solar bound
She to herself herself translated found

The One True Word

Forget honorable and noble
And whatever else you've heard
Bittersweet is the one true word

Forget the heroes and the good
The tragic is absurd
God's dice twinkle when they roll
Bittersweet is the one true word

Beware the wails for those interred
The dead themselves with laughter gird
For bittersweet is the one true word

Beware the sanctimonious breath
The glory it is said they spurred
Mark solemnities or jests—
The medals on their chests
Bittersweet is the one true word
Bittersweet is the one true word

Impediment

Ah, first they said, "Be sensitive."
And then they said "Be tough."
I'll tell you this, I'll tell you what
A man can never be enough

Now the mistress whispers, "Gently."
And the wife she urges, "Rough."
Just give me life, you hollow knife:
A man can never be enough

And now I'm here at sundown.
I'm rid of all my stuff.
Yet even when he's weightless,
A man can never be enough

Don't Brand Me As A War Poet

How's the combat tourism, Phil?

It would be nice to see the soldier out of uniform.

My mom used to use the phrase
"Nor fish nor fowl" a lot.
That amphibious trope has come
To be what I'd say I'd call "Me"
Simply the thing I am shall make me live.
For even in war I wasn't a warrior,
I was a poet masquerading as one.
Even as a soldier I wasn't soldiering.
I never wanted to be a war poet
But I couldn't not be a soldier,
Even if I was a fake one. A fake green beret.
And I can't not be a poet either.
But with the artists I'm a fraudster too
A writer friend told me I write poetry like a soldier,
Asked me to take my uniform off. Do I make you
uncomfortable?
So now I can confirm:
I'm a fake poet too. Maybe I'm too sensitive to be a
poet these days.
So often one is damned to clichés,
If one does or if one doesn't. Maybe I damned myself.
A fake poet dressing up as soldier

A fake soldier dressing up as poet
But my blood and brain were branded by the gods of war,
Uniformed or not. Brand me whatever you will. Heap the coals.
Jingoist. Fake. Singer of war. Listen, I put on your government's clothes,
I went into your cage abroad, the cage so many citizens ignore.
Poet, soldier, neither nor. I was who I was born to be.
Only that and nothing more.

But speak no more of means, medians and modes,
But murmurating angels and their rodes:
Who turned into the sky and culled from air
The traces we called home when we were there.
What's left when we are gone? We cannot say.
Some other soul may ask, some other day.
So we return, and start for the last time
This ultimate rendition of our crime.
And by this rebeginning we shall rend
The myth of finished art. And we will end
As creatures undiminished. We depart:
First forms amid the shadows of the heart.
We limp, pigs' teeth in our ivory shins, poor
As kings in heaven, embers on a winter floor

Language School

Hover through the cypress and the pine
And up the hill you'll find a house of tongues
Where you might hear some syllables divine
Encryptions of the dreams of fallen suns
Where all the words you know are useless sounds
And every something has some other name
Where magic deer still roam the misty grounds
And the voices in your dreams are not the same.
The monarch in the chrysalis is made—
We in our citadel of cryptic jade.
That vortex morphed what lingered of our youths,
Our caterpillar brains and foolish truths.
We fed on fog and language by the sea—
Proficient wings unfurled, we fluttered free

Creation Myth

To sing this song, I need no muse to call,
I was his Lord before I was his thrall;
A tree, a garden and a woman fair
Were first, before that man of earth was there;
Beneath my tree, beside my garden wall,
As I was wont in morning's light to play,
I molded my first man from blood and clay,
When Satan came all bathed in mother's smell,
And with his angel tongue began to tell
Me of the ways and world of things above:
About my mother's kingdom and her love.
He teased me for the little man I'd made
And lingered till the evening light did fade;
He lingered by the garden wall and then
He told me that he'd visit me again

Hallucination

I woke at dusk to take my walk (the day'd
Been long and so to nap myself I'd laid
Beside my tree) and as my way I made
I saw three angels gleaming in a glade:
Hummingbirds beshrouded one whose face
I could not see, with golden claws and grace
She plucked and strummed the strings of some ma-
chine—
And she was clad in glowing armor green.
This hulking vision in the gloam was led
In song by one whose face was red and gold;
The third one, she looked weary, and she read—
Some melancholy had her in its hold.
She did not hear the dark machine's sweet chime,
Only darking vespers of the aftertime

My Executioner

My executioner she waits for me
Beyond the fence and gate behind my home
Amid the snow and empty woods she makes
A quiet circle round a tree

Her heavy blade grows sharper by the year
(She sings in summer when I cannot hear)
Each year she waits till winter patiently,
She then comes circling here around her tree

A menacing indifference in her pace
She waits for me to call her from her place
She waits for me to call her from the snow
To tell her that it's time for us to go

Song

As dimming dusk bled into eve
And birds to roost their whirling ceased
And lightning glittered far away
While thunderheads lurked in the east

An armored knight of greater age
Whose youth was nourished on war's grell
Who'd sucked the smoke of wrath and rage
Was asked to tell of the puzzles of hell

Tell me as this darkness grows
While waiting for our air to come
From whence the source of all things flows
To what amounts the final sum

Tell me something brave and true
Or tell me something grave and light
Of where the tree of knowledge grew
Or whether wrong has ruined right

Tell me as this darkness grows
Of whether we are born to die
Or where's the kingdom of all souls
Or whether brave men cry
Or whether brave men cry

Tell me now that night has come

Of radiances not yet known
Of beauties burning past the sun
Of blazing beings from out our zone
Or tell me when they'll send us home
Tell me when they'll send us home

Tell me this from your abyss
Despite the ruin we have made
Why evil shimmers once it's gone
And beckons from the cancer shade

Or simply tell of good God's ways—
Not why He made this vexing maze—
But why these are the best of days
Why these are the best of days

The Nothing Ground

Mother, Mother what's that sound?
That is the shadow's lullaby
The night song of the nothing ground

Brother, Brother what's that sound?
It is the dirge of a weary world
So weary that it seeks the ground

For though the sun is warm and bright
I cannot slow this drive to night
My doom it shadows every sound
And beckons from the nothing ground

What shimmer from the lightless bound?
What brightness past the deepest ground?
What music hath this nothing sound?
What call from out the nothing ground?

O Brother, Brother the bullet laid you down
Still, beneath the twilight's glow
Your blood was black your skin was snow
Yet now I see you walking round,
An angel of the nothing ground

Praetorian Vesper: Pro Patria

Mine is the quiet plain and pasture
Mine is the catastrophe of suns
Mine is the third god, her light, her laughter:
Each dusk I hear the dirge she hums

Each dawn I see my spangled queen return:
The sheaves the reapers lay beneath her burn

Made in the USA
Monee, IL
24 February 2021

61266349R00025